Happy Halloween, Stinky Face

Written by Lisa McCourt

Illustrated by Cyd Moore

Cartwheel
·B·O·O·K·S· ®

SCHOLASTIC INC.

New York   Toronto   London   Auckland   Sydney
Mexico City   New Delhi   Hong Kong   Buenos Aires

For the amazing peeps on my street~
You make my address my home.
~L.M.

For the spooky Kids in my 'hood!
~C.M.

Library of Congress Cataloging-in-Publication Data available

ISBN-13: 978-0-439-77977-7
ISBN-10: 0-439-77977-4

Text copyright © 2007 by Lisa McCourt.
Illustrations copyright © 2007 by Cyd Moore.
All rights reserved. Published by Scholastic Inc.
SCHOLASTIC, CARTWHEEL BOOKS, and associated logos
are trademarks and/or registered trademarks of Scholastic Inc.

10 9 8 7 6 5 4 3 2 1   07 08 09 10 11

Printed in Singapore

First printing, August 2007

"It's time to get your costume on, Stinky Face!" said Mama.

But I had a question.

doesn't know it's really just

what if she gets so surprised from
her candy bowl up and it lands on

"If Mrs. Petry gets scared,
you'll have to show her
what a nice trick-or-treater
you are. If you say 'please'
and 'thank you' and help
her pick up the candy, she'll
know you're not too terrible."

But, Mama, but, Mama, what if Reese's butterfly costume turns her into a real

Butterfly

and the big wings flap-flap her right up into the sky?

"That would be awesome! She'd get a great view of all her friends in the neighborhood costume parade!"

But, Mama, she won't be able to ring any doorbells if she's flying up in the air. How will she trick-or-treat?

"If Reese's costume turns
her into a real butterfly,
I bet she'll flutter down to
door level to trick-or-treat
with you. Reese loves
candy, you know."

"Oooooooh, if that happens, then Alex the magician will have to wave his magic wand to get the pirates all unstuck."

Brian is going to be a lion, Mama. Lions run really fast. What if he runs so fast that we can't keep up with him to trick-or-treat together?

"Well, isn't Ryan going to be a football player? Football players run very fast, too. Maybe he could catch up and ask the lion to wait for everyone."

But, Mama, Ally is going to be a witch and collect candy in her black cauldro

"If that kind of magic happens, we'll all blow on Ally's cauldron of candy soup to help her cool it off. Then we'll give her a big twisty straw so she can slurp her candy right up!"

Okay, Mama. That's a good idea. But what if Lily Kate, who is a black cat, gets her long tail stuck in the door at one of the houses?

"Firefighters are good at rescuing cats! Maybe Jordan could save her, since he's a firefighter this year."

Scare
D.
Cat

Rest
in
Peace!

Hal.
O.
Ween

But, Mama, but, Mama, what if the candle in our Jack o'Lantern blows out?

What if we accidentally walk into some BIG sticky cobwebs and get all tangled up?

"Lucky for you, Nicholas and Ethan are superheroes. I'm pretty sure superheroes have powers to fix all those problems. So, Stinky Face, let's go have some Halloween fun, okay?"

"I hear your friends coming now. How about this year we stick with your ghost costume, and we'll start worrying first thing tomorrow about what you'll be next year?"

Okay. Happy Halloween, Mama!

"Happy Halloween, my goofy, spooky stinky face."